A JOURNEY TO PARADISE
and *OTHER JEWISH TALES*

Retold by Howard Schwartz
Illustrated by Giora Carmi

FOR SHIRA
NATHAN
AND MIRIAM
AND FOR TSILA

WITH THANKS

Published by Pitspopany Press Copyright © 2000

Text Copyright © 2000 Howard Schwartz

Illustrations Copyright © 2000 Giora Carmi

Design: Tiffen Studios

Cloth   ISBN: 0-943706-21-1
Paper   ISBN: 0-943706-16-5

Pitspopany Press titles may be purchased for fund-raising programs by schools and organizations by contacting:

　　Marketing Director, Pitspopany Press
　　40 East 78th Street, Suite 16D
　　New York, New York 10021
　　Tel: 800-232-2931
　　Fax: 212-472-6253
　　Email: pop@netvision.net.il

Printed in Hong Kong

WHAT'S INSIDE...

A Special Note   5

An Apple From The Tree Of Life   6

King Solomon Tests Fate   14

The Flight Of The Midwife   18

The Heavenly Court   24

A Student In Magic   28

The Finger   32

A Messenger From The World To Come   36

A Journey To Paradise   40

Sources   48

Acknowledgments

Thanks to Arielle North Olson and Susan Menache for their assistance in the editing of these tales.

Thanks too to Professor Dov Noy and Edna Hechal of the Israel Folktale Archives for making the tales of the archives available.

A SPECIAL NOTE
by Howard Schwartz

The Jewish people are known as the People of the Book with good reason. They love to read books, especially the Bible. But they could also be called the People of the Stories, for as they wandered from place to place, they always took their stories with them.

These stories were handed down for many generations until they reached us. Some are more than a thousand years old. One of the best ways to glimpse the Jewish past is in the mirror of these tales. They reveal what was important to the people—what they hoped for, as well as what they feared.

The tales in this book are full of magic. In one tale a rabbi travels to Paradise in search of his best friend, while in another a Jewish girl brings back an enchanted apple from a dream. Some of these stories read like fairy tales, while others are more like ghost stories. In one, King Solomon sends an eagle on a special mission, and in another a foolish boy finds himself married to a corpse.

One of the main reasons these stories were told was to pass down secrets of how to act in difficult situations. The most popular heroine in the tales of the Yemenite Jews was the midwife, who not only helped deliver babies, but also was respected for her wisdom. Here an old midwife is not even afraid of traveling to the kingdom of demons to assist in a birth.

These stories also teach other lessons. Sometimes what we are searching for is not far away, but close at hand, as one student of magic learns the hard way. And sometimes little things—like a sneeze—can come back to haunt us, as one rabbi discovers when his soul tries to enter heaven.

And sometimes these stories are simply meant to make us laugh, like the one about the man who travels to the city of Chelm and pretends to be a messenger from the dead.

Here are eight stories from around the world—not only from Eastern Europe, but also from Tunisia, Yemen and Israel. Each one has traveled a long way, and now it is time for them to be retold.

AN APPLE FROM THE TREE OF LIFE

The daughter of the Sultan of Turkey had fallen ill. Not even the finest doctors in all of Istanbul could heal her. The sultan brought them together and asked them when she would recover. One after another, the doctors hung their heads and said, "I don't know." But the very last doctor said, "Nothing can help her now except for an apple from the Tree of Life."

"What apple is that?" the sultan demanded to know. "And where can it be found?"

The last doctor said, "I have only heard of such an apple. But surely it can be found in the Garden of Eden. Two trees are said to grow in the center of the garden. The Tree of Life is one of them, and the Tree of Knowledge is the other. It is said that whoever tastes an apple from the Tree of Life, no matter how ill he may be, will recover his health."

The eyes of the sultan grew wide. "I must obtain one of these enchanted apples," the sultan said. "Who knows where this garden can be found?"

"Those who know best about the garden," the doctor replied, "are the Jews. What we know about the garden is told in the Bible. That is the holiest book of the Jews."

The face of the sultan grew red. "Bring in the leaders of the Jews at once!" he shouted.

Before an hour had passed, three of the best-known rabbis of the city stood before the sultan, wondering why they had been summoned on such short notice.

"As you know," the sultan said, looking very grim, "my daughter is deathly ill. Her only hope is something that is in your power to supply, and supply it you must. For if you fail, my wrath will fall upon you."

"Your Majesty," one of the rabbis said, "you know that we will gladly do whatever we can. But what do you want us to do?"

"Know then," said the sultan, "that I need an apple from the Tree of Life. And I need it soon—within three days. If I don't have it by then, you and all of your people will be banished!"

And the sultan dismissed the three rabbis with a wave of his hand.

The three rabbis discussed the matter among themselves, and they all agreed that what the sultan was asking for was simply impossible. No one knew where the Garden of Eden could be found. And even if they did, how could anyone go there and come back within three days?

So the leaders gathered all the people in the synagogues, and they went from one synagogue to another, telling them the terrible news. All the people despaired, for no one believed it would be possible to obtain an enchanted apple from the Tree of Life in such a short time.

Now one of the three rabbis who had met with the sultan had a daughter named Leah. How she wished that such a wondrous apple could be found, so that the sultan's daughter could recover, and the danger to all the Jews would disappear.

Leah saw that her father was deeply worried by the sultan's demands, so she said, "Surely, Father, we must not give up hope. Miracles have happened before. Let us pray for one to happen to us. Tell me, is there anyone who knows the way to the Garden of Eden?"

"Only the thirty-six righteous ones," her father replied. "But no one knows where they can be found."

"But, Father," Leah said, "I have heard of an old Jew who lives alone in the forest. It is whispered that he might be one of the thirty-six."

Now the rabbi remembered that he, too, had heard such things said about this old man. So he and his daughter set out at once to look for him.

It was not easy to find their way through the forest, but everyone did their best to assist the rabbi and his daughter, and finally they reached the old man's house. They knocked on his door, and when he opened it, Leah was astonished to see that there was a light surrounding his face.

The old man listened carefully as the rabbi explained what the sul-

tan had demanded of them. Then he went to a shelf, took down an ancient book, and opened it. There, pressed in its pages, was a green leaf, perfectly preserved.

The old man took the leaf in his hand. "This leaf has been pressed between the pages of this book for many centuries. It is said to have been picked from one of the trees in the Garden of Eden. Let your daughter place this leaf on her pillow and she will dream of that glorious garden."

"My daughter?" asked the astonished rabbi.

"Yes," said the old man. "For she is the one destined to journey there."

Neither Leah nor her father could believe their good fortune, yet they were mystified that the old man had given the precious leaf to Leah instead of to the rabbi. Still, they both thanked the old man and set out to return to their home.

On their way, Leah and her father stopped at an inn, and before she went to sleep, Leah gently placed the ancient leaf on her pillow. Even though it was so very old, it looked as fresh as if it had been picked that very day. It also gave off a most wonderful scent that filled the room. Bathed in that beautiful scent, Leah closed her eyes, and soon she was sound asleep.

In her dream, Leah found herself in the most splendid Garden she had ever seen. Every kind of fruit tree grew there, and the whole garden was filled with a beautiful, unforgettable scent. Leah suddenly realized that she had indeed traveled to the Garden of Eden. She knew that she must hurry, she must find the Tree of Life before it was too late. Tomorrow was the last day the sultan had given them to bring back the enchanted apple.

Leah looked up and saw that there was an angel sleeping in every tree. She called out to one, and when the angel opened its eyes, she asked for its help in finding the Tree of Life. The angel agreed to serve as her guide, but told her that it could take her only to the center of the garden. She would have to figure out for herself which of the two trees that grew there was the Tree of Life.

With the angel's help, Leah soon found herself in the center of that wonderful garden. There two trees grew, each a mirror image of the other. Apples hung from the branches of both trees. She looked from one tree to the other for a clue as to which was the Tree of Life. But which one should she choose?

Then Leah happened to notice a serpent hidden in the branches of one of the trees, and she was certain that must be the Tree of Knowledge.

Without further hesitation, she plucked a ripe apple from the other tree, and in the same instant, she woke up.

Leah opened her eyes, surprised to find herself back in the inn. Then she saw it—a ripe and shining apple resting on her pillow right where the fragrant leaf had been. An apple from the Tree of Life! Somehow

she had brought it back in her dream. Leah could barely believe her eyes. She realized that a miracle had truly taken place, and she jumped up, grabbed the apple, and showed it to her father, who had not slept a wink. His eyes opened wide when he saw it, and even wider when she told him her dream. He shed tears of joy, for now he knew that they could still be saved.

Wasting not a moment, they set out for the sultan's palace, and when they arrived, the rabbi presented the sultan with the apple. When the sultan saw the rabbi's joy, he, too, was overjoyed. He himself brought the fragrant apple to his ailing daughter, and held it beneath her nose. All at once she opened her eyes. Then he asked her to take a bite of it, and as soon as she did, the color returned to her face, and she sat up. Within the hour she had made a miraculous recovery.

The sultan hugged his daughter and declared that day to be a holiday for all. Then the sultan publicly thanked the Jews for saving her, and never again did he threaten them.

As for Leah and her father, the sultan invited them to live in the palace, and Leah and the sultan's daughter became the best of friends. Leah never tired of telling her about her astonishing dream, and about the enchanted apple she had brought back. The sultan's daughter never tired of hearing this tale, for she, better than anyone else, knew that every word was true.

Eastern Europe: Nineteenth Century

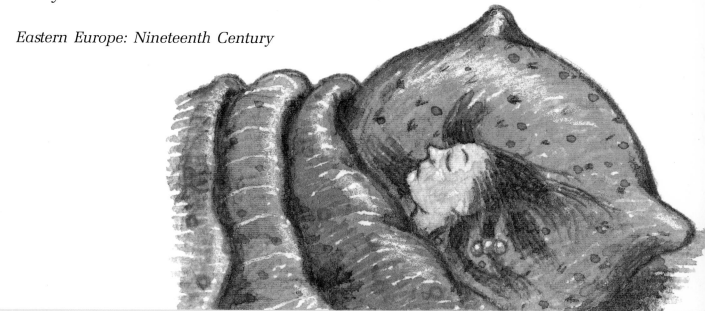

KING SOLOMON TESTS FATE

King Solomon, the wisest of all men, knew not only the languages of the birds, the animals, and the winds. He could also hear the voices of angels as they whispered among themselves.

Once King Solomon heard the angels discussing a certain girl. They said she was destined to marry a certain young man. King Solomon wondered if anything could prevent this match from taking place, and he decided to put fate to the test.

King Solomon summoned an eagle. When it arrived, he said, "I want you to carry a certain girl to the desert and guard her there. Don't bring her back until you are ordered to do so. Take whatever food she needs from the palace."

The eagle did as King Solomon commanded. One day, while the girl was walking in a field, the eagle swooped down, picked her up, and carried her away to the desert. He took her to a cave, and every day he brought her two loaves of bread and other provisions from the palace.

Now it happened that there was a certain young man who set sail from a distant land by himself. While he was out at sea, his boat was captured by a powerful wind and wrecked upon an unknown shore.

The young man was grateful to have survived, and he set out to find his way back home. As he was crossing the desert, suddenly a windstorm struck. The sand stung his face and almost blinded him, so he sought shelter in the nearest cave, and that was the very cave in which the girl was being held.

When the eagle arrived with the provisions that day, it discovered there were two people staying in the cave. After that, the eagle brought enough food for them both.

Before very long, the two fell in love and decided to get married. The eagle was the only witness at their wedding.

As the years passed, the couple had five sons and daughters. To feed them all, the eagle had to bring large amounts of food. King Solomon noticed this, and he called upon the eagle. "Tell me, why is it you are emptying entire storerooms of food from the palace? I commanded you to look after only one person."

The eagle said, "You told me to look after one person, but now there are seven."

King Solomon was astonished. "How has this come to pass?" he asked.

The eagle told the king how the young man had come to the cave, and how he and the girl had married and become the parents of five children.

Then King Solomon ordered the eagle to bring the family to the palace. The eagle did so. When they arrived, the young man told the king how the wind had carried him so far from home, and how he had met the love of his life in that distant cave.

Then King Solomon, the wisest of all men, understood that fate had found a way to bring the couple together after all. He gave them his blessings, as well as a fine house of their own, and they lived together in joy and peace all the days of their lives.

Tunisia: Oral Tradition

THE FLIGHT OF THE MIDWIFE

There once was an old midwife who lived in the land of Yemen. She had helped at the births of so many children that she had lost count of them. Still, when the time came for a child to be born, the people of her village trusted her more than anyone else.

Now the midwife was not only a grandmother, but a great-grandmother as well. God had blessed her with good health. Every day she loved to take a long walk in the forest not far from her little house. She had a favorite place—a clearing where all kinds of birds gathered, and she was familiar with every one of them. But one day, just as the old woman reached that clearing, she heard the cawing of a bird she did not recognize. She was surprised, and she peered into the trees, trying to find out which bird it was. There, perched on a low branch, she saw the blackest, shiniest raven she had ever seen.

Now the midwife felt certain that there was something strange about the bird, so she stared hard at it. And it stared right back at her. Suddenly the raven began to speak.

"Greetings, Grandmother. I have come here in search of you."

The midwife had seen a great many things in her long life, but a speaking bird was not one of them. Still, she was too old to be surprised by anything.

"What is it you want?" she asked.

"Your fame as a midwife has traveled farther than you think," the bird said. "Your assistance is needed in our land. I want you to accompany me."

The old midwife wasn't the least bit afraid. "I have never hesitated when called upon to assist in a birth," she said. "But you have come here from far away. How can I get there? I am an old woman."

The bird replied, "You can fly back with me."

"How is that possible?" she asked.

In a wink, the bird brushed her forehead with its wing, and an instant later the old woman found herself flying above the highest trees in that forest and up into the sky. With the raven leading the way, they flew for so long that she saw the sun set and the moon rise before they reached the land that was their destination.

When it seemed as if they had flown around the world, the raven began to descend into a dense forest. The midwife did her best to follow. It glided in and out of the branches and so, somehow, did she.

At last the raven flew through a hole in a tree. "What should I do?" the midwife cried out as she approached that tiny opening.

"Keep going!" came the voice of the raven from inside the trunk. And she did.

Now no sooner did she pass through the opening, than the midwife found herself inside a mansion fit for a king. The walls were made of marble, and there were gold and silver objects everywhere.

A distinguished looking gentleman stood before her.

"Who are you?" she asked.

"I am the raven," he replied.

"How can that be?" the midwife asked.

"Did you not fly here and pass through a hole in the tree smaller than your fist?"

The midwife nodded.

"Know, then, that this is the Kingdom of Demons. I have brought you here because my wife is about to give birth, and she needs you."

"Of course," said the midwife, who was always willing to help bring a newborn into the world.

So she went into the room where the demon's wife lay. The beautiful young demoness, with long, dark hair, was very happy to see that the midwife had arrived in time to help her.

Now that was the midwife's first delivery of a demon. It took all her skill to make sure that the birth went well. Soon a baby demon was born.

When mother and infant were safely resting, the noble demon thanked the midwife and hung a large ring of garlic cloves around her neck.

"This will serve you well when you arrive home," he said.

Then the demon turned back into a raven before her eyes, and said, "Follow me."

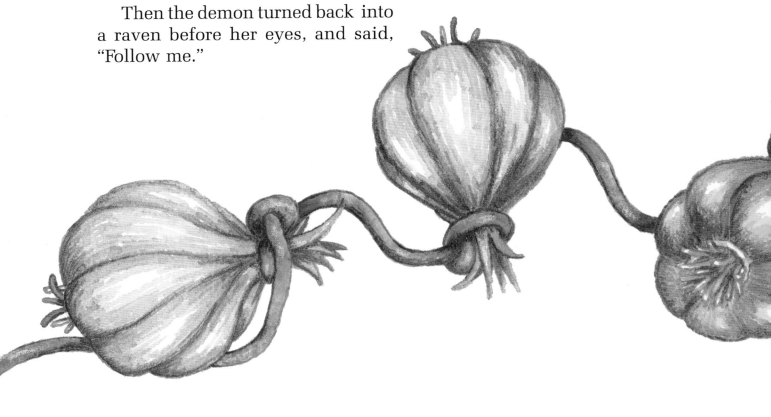

All at once, the midwife found herself flying through the heavens once again. This time, though, the journey was completed in the blink of an eye. All at once the midwife found herself standing before her own house. The raven was nowhere to be seen.

That is when she discovered that the garlic necklace she was wearing had turned to the purest gold.

Yemen: Oral Tradition

THE HEAVENLY COURT

It was as well known in heaven as it was on earth that Rabbi Yitzhak of Berditchev delighted in the Sabbath. On that day he rested his body as well as his soul. Nor did he do work of any kind, for that is forbidden on the day of rest.

When the pious Rabbi Levi Yitzhak died, there was a great uproar in the heavenly court. For the prosecuting angel argued that Rabbi Levi Yitzhak had once broken the Sabbath, and therefore his soul should be denied a portion in the World to Come.

But none of the angels believed Rabbi Levi Yitzhak would ever break the Sabbath. So they demanded to know exactly what the rabbi had done.

The prosecuting angel explained that one Sabbath afternoon, when Rabbi Levi Yitzhak was speaking to his Hasidim, two horses were standing outside, hitched to a carriage. All at once Rabbi Levi Yitzhak sneezed so loudly he startled the horses. They leapt forward, breaking the Sabbath, for no traveling is permitted on that day. Even causing someone else's carriage to move is not allowed.

Now the uproar in the heavenly court grew even louder. One after another, angels came forward and defended the rabbi from the charge of the prosecuting angel. They insisted his soul was still pure, because he had not intended to drive the horses forward. Therefore he had not broken the Sabbath.

Many of Rabbi Levi Yitzhak's followers, who were already in heaven, also came forward to defend him. They reported all the good deeds he had performed. And there was not a single bad thing they had to say about him.

Still, the prosecuting angel continued to insist that he be kept out of heaven.

Then Rabbi Levi Yitzhak himself, who was the very soul of fairness, asked to speak. He said that he was inclined to agree with the prosecuting angel, that it was indeed his fault. After all, his sneeze had caused the horses to bolt.

Just then God's voice came forth from on high. "Has my son Levi Yitzhak arrived yet? I have been awaiting him." The prosecuting angel grew very pale and quiet. And the soul of Rabbi Levi Yitzhak was welcomed into heaven with much celebrating in the World to Come.

Israel: Oral Tradition

A STUDENT IN MAGIC

There once was a young Jewish student who wanted to study magic. A wandering magician had passed through his town one day and taught him a few tricks, but he wanted to learn more. He heard that in a far-off land there was a great sorcerer, and he decided to go there to study with him.

On the third day of his travels, he stopped at an inn. The innkeeper asked him where he was going, and when the young man told him, the innkeeper said, "Must you go so far? Stay here with me, and I will teach you magic."

Now the student found it hard to believe that the innkeeper was really a magician. He did not look or act like one. So he politely refused the innkeeper's offer.

The innkeeper said, "So be it. I won't try to stop you. But you have been traveling a long time. Why don't you go to the well in back of the inn and wash?"

The student was hot and dusty, so he went to the well and lowered the bucket. When he brought it up, he splashed water on his face. But when he opened his eyes, the well had vanished and the inn was nowhere to be seen. Instead he found himself standing alone on a dock, where a ship was about to set sail.

Afraid of being left behind, the young man boarded the ship. After several weeks, it arrived in a beautiful city. The young man left the boat and wandered through the streets. Everywhere he went, the people seemed very sad, and the young man wondered why.

At last he learned that the princess of that land could not stop crying. Her pet bird had died, and no one could console her. The king had announced that whoever made her laugh again could marry the princess and receive half the king's wealth. But anyone who failed would lose his head.

When the young man heard this, he went directly to the palace and offered to try his luck. The young man was taken to her room, where he saw her sobbing into her pillow. What could he do? All he knew were a few magic tricks. So he decided to show them to the princess.

"Watch closely," the young man told her. Then he pronounced a spell, and a white bird appeared out of nowhere. The princess watched in amazement as the bird flew around the room.

After that he pronounced another spell, and a white rose appeared out of thin air.

Finally, the young man pronounced a third spell, and the bird snatched the rose out of his hand and took it to the princess, dropping it in her lap. The princess began to laugh out loud. The magic bird delighted her, and she cried no more.

When the king learned that the princess had stopped crying, he was overjoyed. The wedding of the princess and the young man soon took place. And so it was that the young man became a member of the royal family.

Now as time passed the king came to trust the young man, and often sent him on important missions. Once it was necessary for the young man to journey by ship to reach a distant city. So he took leave of the princess and set sail.

When the ship had been at sea for only seven days, a great storm arose. The ship was tossed from side to side, and all at once it was struck by lightning and quickly sank. Of all those on the ship, only the young man survived.

For three days and nights he clung to a plank and was carried by the currents. Eventually, the waves carried him close to an island. With the last of his strength, he managed to swim to shore.

As he lay there, exhausted, he heard a voice say, "What is keeping you so long? If you don't hurry, your food will get cold." The young man looked up in amazement and saw the innkeeper standing over him. Then he noticed that he was lying on the ground next to a well. Nearby he saw the inn he had stopped at so long ago.

When the innkeeper saw his confusion, he said, "It was my magic that made you imagine all these things. In fact, everything was an illusion. Only an hour has passed since you went to the well. Now you see that you don't have to travel to distant lands to learn magic. Remain with me and I will teach you."

And he did.

Eastern Europe: Nineteenth Century

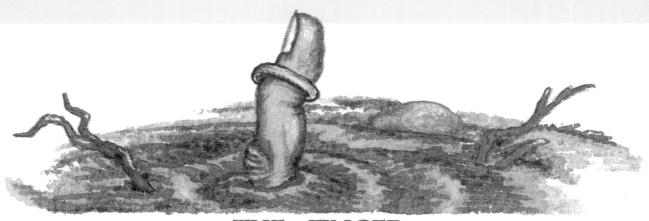

THE FINGER

Three young men walked along a river bank near the city of Safed, laughing and joking, for tomorrow was Samuel's wedding day.

Samuel was in such a playful mood that he picked up a stone and flung it across the moonlit water. It skipped on the surface seven times before it sank.

"I'm lucky tonight," he said, and he reached down for another stone but his hand brushed against something like a twig sticking out of the dirt.

"What's that?" he asked, peering at it in the pale moonlight. "A finger," said one of his friends, laughing.

"A finger in need of a ring," said the other.

"And I happen to have a ring," said Samuel. "Will you two witness my wedding?"

He pulled off his ring with a flourish and slipped it onto what he thought was a twig sticking out of the ground. Then he grinned and practiced his wedding vow, repeating it three times: "With these words, I thee wed."

But the moment he finished, the twig began to twitch. All at once a hand rose up out of the earth. And suddenly the corpse of a woman stood up, wearing a worm-eaten shroud. The young men jumped back in horror just as she opened her arms and cried "My husband!"

The friends were terrified. They ran back along the river bank, bumping into trees, cutting themselves on bushes, and all the while they heard the corpse screaming close behind them.

Finally they reached the house of study, rushed inside and locked the door. For a long time they were too frightened to speak. When they

calmed down, they decided never to tell anyone what had happened.

The next morning, when the bride and groom were standing together under the wedding canopy, just as they were about to say the wedding vows, suddenly there was a bloodcurdling scream from the back of the crowd. People started running in every direction, for standing there was the same corpse, wearing the same worm-eaten shroud.

"He can't marry her," she shouted. "He's already married to me!"

By then, everyone had run out of the synagogue except for the corpse, and Samuel and the rabbi. Samuel was trying to hide himself behind the rabbi.

"Tell me, woman," said the rabbi, "why have you left the dead and returned to the living?"

"Because last night he became my husband." And she held up her hand with Samuel's ring on it and pointed directly at him.

The rabbi turned to Samuel. "Is what she says true?"

"It's...it's true," he said, "but we were only teasing. We saw this thing sticking out of the earth...I put my ring on it...and said the words..."

"Were there two witnesses?" asked the rabbi.

"Yes," Samuel whispered.

"Then we must convene a court of rabbis."

Word quickly spread through the city of Safed that Samuel might be

married to a corpse. For Samuel had married her according to the law. Yet what could they do about it?

And so it was that the court was held in the synagogue. The corpse came forth and testified that Samuel had put the ring on her finger willingly, and his friends reluctantly admitted that they had witnessed the ceremony.

But Samuel's father said he had vowed to betroth his son to the daughter of his friend many years earlier—and they should be wed as planned.

And the father of the bride agreed, saying that this betrothal had been agreed upon even before the children were born.

After the rabbis had conferred with one another, they called forth the corpse. She stood before the congregation in her worm-eaten shroud, and they all shrank back in fear.

"Would you be willing," the rabbis asked, "to free this man of the vow he made?"

"No," she said. "I never married in my life. I want my hour of joy. I want him to be my husband."

Samuel sat with his head in his hands, crying and shaking.

Then the rabbis announced their decision. "Samuel wed this corpse according to the letter of the law, but the vow was made in jest. Besides, his betrothal was made prior to this vow. According to Jewish law, an earlier vow may not be canceled by a later one. Therefore we declare that Samuel's marriage to the corpse is not valid."

At that moment the corpse let forth a bloodcurdling shriek and dropped dead once more.

"Take her body and give her a proper funeral," the rabbis said. "And this time make sure she is buried very deep."

Palestine: 17th Century

A MESSENGER FROM THE WORLD TO COME

There once was a poor Jew named Moshe who had twelve children to feed and clothe. But he had no job, and he had so many troubles that neither he nor his wife was able to sleep at night. Winter was coming, and they had no wood for a fire, nor did they have any warm clothes for themselves or for their children. The poor man did not know where to look for help, and meanwhile winter was coming that much closer every day.

Now the town where Moshe lived was not very far from the town of Chelm. Although he had never been there, Moshe had heard stories about the inhabitants of Chelm all his life. They were said to be very gullible. It was even whispered that they were fools. So, out of desperation, Moshe decided to trick the inhabitants of Chelm.

First Moshe took all of his savings and rented a wagon. Then he drove the wagon to the cemetery outside of Chelm, where he studied the names inscribed on the tombstones. Next he drove to the marketplace, where he announced that he had brought tidings to the people of Chelm from the World to Come.

Naturally this news was a great surprise to the people. Many visitors had passed through their city, but none from the World to Come. That was where people went when they died, but no one had ever come back. So the people of Chelm they were truly amazed to learn that such a visitor had come their way. A large crowd soon gathered, and before long every man, woman, and child stood around Moshe and stared at him in amazement.

Then Moshe named the ones who were sending greetings from the World to Come, using the same names he had read on the tombstones.

The people of Chelm were astounded. Then Moshe told the people of Chelm that he had also brought a request from them: winter was coming in the World to Come as well as in this one, and the shrouds of the departed were not enough to keep them warm. Nor did they have wood to build their fires. Thus they had sent this messenger from the World to Come to ask that all of these things be sent.

Naturally the people of Chelm did not want to deny the necessities of life to those who had moved from this world to the next. They all hurried home and came back with everything their relatives would need—coats and sweaters of every kind, and a huge pile of wood that completely filled up Moshe's wagon. Moshe thanked them for their generosity with all his heart, and he set off to deliver the gifts to those in the World to Come.

And that is how Moshe managed to fill his house that winter with everything his family needed. In this way they survived that winter without difficulty, and they were not forced to go from this world to the next before their time.

Israel: Oral Tradition

A JOURNEY TO PARADISE

There once were two rabbis who spent countless hours together, sharing secrets of the Torah, and sometimes just sitting in silence. One always knew what the other was thinking, for they were as close as twin brothers.

One of these rabbis was the Kotzker Rebbe and the other was his good friend, Reb Yitzhak of Vorki. Whenever they were apart, they sent each other letters by messenger. That way they never lost contact, and their friendship continued to flourish.

Then it happened that Reb Yitzhak died, and his soul ascended to heaven, leaving the Kotzker Rebbe behind. The Kotzker Rebbe was deeply grieved by the loss of his friend. Yet he felt certain that even though Reb Yitzhak had left this world, somehow they would remain in touch. He expected Reb Yitzhak to contact him from heaven, just as he had always sent him letters when they were apart. Perhaps he would come to him in a dream, or find some other way to contact him from the World to Come.

But a week passed and there was no sign from Reb Yitzhak, not even a dream. Still the Kotzker Rebbe was certain he would be hearing from him. But when a month had passed, the Kotzker Rebbe began to worry about his friend, even though he was no longer among the living. He thought to himself, "Well, if he won't come to me, then I'll go to him."

So the Kotzker Rebbe decided to ascend to Paradise, to search for his friend, Reb Yitzhak. One night, when all of his Yeshiva students were asleep, he pronounced the Holy Name and his soul flew up to heaven.

He found himself standing before the palace of the sage Maimonides, also known as the Rambam. For all of the great prophets and sages have their own palaces in the World to Come, where they continue to teach. He entered there and saw that thousands of angels and the souls of the righteous had gathered to hear the Rambam speak on the Torah. The Kotzker Rebbe took a seat in the back row and listened with great joy to the teachings of Maimonides.

When the Rambam finished teaching, the Kotzer Rebbe made his way to him and embraced him and thanked him for all that he had taught him. Then he told Maimonides that he was on a mission to find Reb Yitzhak of Vorki, and he asked if he had seen him. "Ah, Reb Yitzhak—what a teacher he is!" the Rambam said. "He taught us wonderful secrets of the Torah. Yes, he was here—but he left."

So the Kotzker Rebbe took his leave of Maimonides, and he ascended higher into heaven, all the way to the palace of Rashi. There too he found thousands of sages and angels gathered at the feet of Rashi, listening carefully as the great commentator enlightened them about the secrets of the Torah.

When Rashi had finished his lesson, the Kotzker Rebbe came to him and thanked him for all that he had taught him. Then he asked him if he had seen Reb Yitzhak.

"Ah, Reb Yitzhak!" said Rashi. "It was he who taught me how to read between the lines of the Torah to find the secrets hidden there. He is the master of masters! Yes, he was here—but he left."

So the Kotzker Rebbe took his leave of Rashi and ascended even higher into heaven, all the way to the palace of Moshe Rabbenu, our teacher Moses. There he saw that thousands had gathered to hear the words of Moses, and soon he, too, heard the Torah taught from the very lips of Moses. He thought to himself that it was so wonderful that he would like to remain there forever. But then he remembered his mission.

So when Moses had finished, the Kotzker Rebbe went to him, weeping, and thanked him for the eternal blessing of the Torah that Moses had brought to the Jewish people. And Moses said, "Rebbe, we have known about you in heaven for a long time. Look, we have even been saving a place for you. Have you come to join us?"

"No," said the Kotzker Rebbe, "not yet. I am on a mission to find Reb Yitzhak of Vorki. Tell me, have you seen him?"

"Ah, Reb Yitzhak!" said Moses. "You know, I thought I had learned everything there was to know about the Torah at Mount Sinai, but Reb Yitzhak showed me how much more there is to learn. Yes, he was here—but he left."

So the Kotzker Rebbe reluctantly took his leave of Moses and ascended even higher, into the highest heaven of all. There he found himself before the palace of Avraham Avinu, our father Abraham. He went inside and once again he saw that thousands of angels and the souls of the righteous had gathered to hear the Torah taught from the lips of Abraham. The Kotzker Rebbe marveled at how clear Abraham's voice was, and how brightly his eyes shone. He realized that he had longed all his life to be in the presence of Abraham, and now that he was, how could he tear himself away? But then he remembered Reb Yitzhak, and he knew that he could not rest until he had found him.

So when Abraham had finished speaking, the Kotzker Rebbe went to him, kissed his hands, and thanked him for all the great blessings that he had brought to the Jews. And Abraham embraced him and said,

"You, too, Rebbe, have brought great honor to your people. How can I help you?"

Then the Kotzker Rebbe poured out his heart to Abraham, and told him how close he was to his friend, Reb Yitzhak, and how much he had missed him since he had taken leave of the world. He asked Abraham if Reb Yitzhak had been there.

"Of course he was here!" said Abraham. "He is a wonderful teacher. He taught us how to read the white letters hidden in the spaces between the black letters of the Torah. We will never forget all that he taught us. But, I am sorry to say, he left."

"Please, father Abraham," the Kotzker Rebbe pleaded. "Tell me where I can find him."

And Abraham said: "If you wish to find him, then here is what you must do: You must go back to the world you came from and travel to the ends of the earth. There you will find a dark forest that will seem to be endless. Somehow you must make your way through that forest, and if you do, there you will find Reb Yitzhak."

The Kotzker Rebbe wept when he learned this secret. He embraced Abraham and reluctantly took his leave. He returned to this world and traveled to the very ends of the earth. There he found the dark forest that Abraham had spoken of, but it was much longer and darker than he had imagined. It seemed to take him twenty years to make his way through that forest, but at last the forest came to an end, and there he saw a great ocean.

Now when the Kotzker Rebbe stared at that ocean, he could barely believe his eyes. It was not like any other ocean he had ever seen. Its waters rose up almost to heaven, and as they rose up and fell back, there was the sound of sighing and moaning. What kind of ocean was this? Just then, the Kotzker Rebbe saw Reb Yitzhak standing by the shore of that ocean, leaning on a staff.

"Yitzhak! Yitzhak!" he cried, running to him.

"Mendel," Reb Yitzhak replied, "Mendel, come here!"

Then, at last, they were together, and they embraced and wept. Then Reb Yitzhak said, "Mendel, do you know what ocean this is?"

Once again the Kotzker Rebbe turned to that strange ocean, saw how high the waves rose up, heard its sighing, and said, "No, I do not. Tell me, what ocean is this?"

And Reb Yitzhak said, "This is the Ocean of Tears, of all the tears shed by the Jews. The waves of this ocean reach up to heaven, pleading for mercy, then they fall back to earth. And I swore to God that I wouldn't move from here until God dried all the tears!"

Then the Kotzker Rebbe understood why he had not heard from his friend since he had departed from the world, for Reb Yitzhak had indeed taken on a great task. The Kotzker Rebbe turned to Reb Yitzhak and said, "I can think of no greater mission than this. But I cannot bear to be without you. So let me join you here, and together we will pray together until God dries every tear."

And some say that they are still standing there, imploring God to dry those tears and to bring peace, at last, to the Jewish people.

Eastern Europe: Oral Tradition

SOURCES

AN APPLE FROM THE TREE OF LIFE (Eastern Europe)
From *Dos Bukh fun Nissyoynes*, edited by Israel Osman. Los Angeles: 1926

KING SOLOMON TESTS FATE (Tunisia)
Israel Folktale Archives 3264, collected by Binyamin Mazouz from Marcel Mazouz. From *Shiv'im Sipurim ve-Sipur mi-Pi Yehude Tunisya*, edited by Dov Noy, #54. Jerusalem: 1966.

THE FLIGHT OF THE MIDWIFE (Yemen)
Israel Folktale Archives 13676, collected by Hadara Sela from her mother, Rachel Tzabari.

THE HEAVENLY COURT (Israel)
Israel Folktale Archives 4941, collected by Esther Weinstein from Rabbi Moshe Weinstein. From *Savta Esther Mesaperet*, edited by Zippora Kagan. Haifa: 1964.

A STUDENT IN MAGIC (Eastern Europe)
From *Volksliteratur der Ostjuden,* edited by Immanuel Olsvanger. Basel: 1931.

THE FINGER (Israel)
From *Shivhei ha-Ari*, compiled by Shlomo Meinsterl. Jerusalem: 1905.

A MESSENGER FROM THE WORLD TO COME (Israel)
Israel Folktale Archives 2826, collected by Esther Weinstein from Rabbi Hayim Zaltz. From *Savta Esther Mesaperet,* edited by Zippora Kagan. Haifa: 1964.

A JOURNEY TO PARADISE (Eastern Europe)
Collected by Howard Schwartz from Rabbi Shlomo Carlebach.